T0086360

I CAN'T
HEAR
THE MUSIC

H. WASHINGTEN

I CAN'T HEAR THE MUSIC

Copyright © 2020 H. Washingten.

All rights reserved. No part of this book may be used or reproduced by any means, graphic, electronic, or mechanical, including photocopying, recording, taping or by any information storage retrieval system without the written permission of the author except in the case of brief quotations embodied in critical articles and reviews.

iUniverse books may be ordered through booksellers or by contacting:

iUniverse
1663 Liberty Drive
Bloomington, IN 47403
www.iuniverse.com
844-349-9409

Because of the dynamic nature of the Internet, any web addresses or links contained in this book may have changed since publication and may no longer be valid. The views expressed in this work are solely those of the author and do not necessarily reflect the views of the publisher, and the publisher hereby disclaims any responsibility for them.

Any people depicted in stock imagery provided by Getty Images are models, and such images are being used for illustrative purposes only.
Certain stock imagery © Getty Images.

ISBN: 978-1-6632-0116-4 (sc)
ISBN: 978-1-6632-0117-1 (e)

Print information available on the last page.

iUniverse rev. date: 12/15/2020

ACKNOWLEDGEMENTS

First, I want to thank God. He is the one who has given me this talent. It is because of you that I can do this with joy. Thank you to my husband who encourages me, let me cry, hold my hand, tell me the truth when I don't want to hear it. I LOVE YOU! Thank you, to my daughter for being my motivation. I am thankful for God giving you to me. I love you so much. It seems so unreal to love someone this much unconditionally. To my parents, thank you for all you've done. To my family, far, near, and extended I love you. I am thankful, grateful to everyone who has encouraged and sown into my life. I thank you all!

PROLOGUE

Everyone does not look at life the same but love don't judge who you are. I count that a blessing at times. Most of all I am glad God still loves me after all the things I have done. The Bible states He only can judge because no one is perfect. Jesus said who without sin cast the first stone. I'm glad I can't! When I get the eyes of 'you are below me', I ask the question who made you judge?

My name is Promise Halley Goodman. I was fourteen when my life took a drastic change. My passion for music went with my innocence and childhood until I learned how to take my passion for music to express my pain. My mom was my best friend. It was me and her for a long time before we moved from South Carolina to North Carolina. My father didn't treat my Mom and me like we should have been treated. Yes, he did work and provide. He was an emotional earthquake though. That is the best way I can explain it. Mom got tired of my Dad. She finally left when I was seven. I had no respect for my Dad at all. When they were living together my Mom made me call him Dad. When I wasn't around Mom I called him Arnold. Yes, when I learned his name, I laughed so hard I felt my stomach burning. By the way, he answered to me calling him Arnold. When I had to stay with Arnold during his time which was every other weekend, he would always take me to visit my grandma, Halley. Grandma was glad that Mom left Dad. She would apologize to me and Mom when she'd see us because she felt she went wrong somewhere with Dad. Grandma would say "I did the best I knew how. During my time being a single Mom was looked upon as shameful, we were made to be ashamed. Please, tell me where young girls respect for themselves has gone to?"

This was a ritual question. I couldn't answer because I was still learning myself. If Grandma was still with me I could answer that question now. I enjoyed my visits with Grandma. As I got older I would avoid Arnold and have my Mom drop me off to Grandma. Grandma would get excited to know I was coming for the weekend. It broke my heart when she would cry when I left. I didn't have any idea what was happening back at home. I was thinking Mom was enjoying her break away from me. This bastard named Leyon Bromdestin was a preacher of the local church about two miles from our house. Leyon was a sheep to everyone else but a wolf at home. He had the whole community fooled except Ms. Lou. Ms. Lou didn't care about Leyon's title of being the pastor at Second Street Tabernacle. Ms. Lou said "if he is an asshole now. He will be an asshole until Jesus changes him." Leyon tried to intimidate Ms. Lou when Mom went to her for help or advice. Leyon had beat Mom so bad one weekend she couldn't go to church because she was in so much pain. The other reason was 'cause make-up couldn't hide that black eye. Mom went to visit Ms. Lou to get out of the house. My Mom's name is Trisha. Ms. Lou would call her Tis. I tried to figure out for years where r, h, and the a went in her name. Ms. Lou had her own language. Her language was very clear when she was cussing you out. She would say S.O.B so clear you woulda thought it was the proper English language. Ms. Lou helped my Mom to come up with a plan to leave Leyon. Leyon figured it out so he didn't realize Ms. Lou was crazy on top of crazy. She could have got a check if someone evaluated her closely. Anyway, the plan was three months from being completed until someone in the neighborhood told Leyon they saw Trisha at Ms. Lou's house. That day replays in my mind like it was yesterday. Mom had just got home from work. I had just gotten home from my best friend Leah house. I was sitting on the sofa watching the six o'clock news. Mom was trying to get dinner started. Leyon walks in the back door that leads into the kitchen. Mom's back was turned towards him. He grabs her hair which was in a ponytail. "Why were you over to Lou Gee's house?" yelled Leyon. Mom was just so shocked she had to think quickly before he punched her. "She asked me the next time I made some soup to bring her some. I was just being nice and taking her a bowl of soup, Leyon." Mom's voice was shaky but she held it together. Leyon knew something wasn't right about that visit. He let Mom's hair go without throwing her head around. I was scared he was going to break her neck. He walks out the kitchen door, and slams the door so hard until the glass shakes. I automatically ran to the phone to call Ms. Lou. Our code for Leyon's was two rings. Ms. Lou kept her gun ready. Leyon was banging on the door so hard our next-door neighbor the Peter's came out of their home looking and trying to see what was going on. Leyon's anger exploded when she didn't answer the door. When Leyon kicked that door in, Ms. Lou put a bullet in his knee and shoulder. She told the police that he broke in. Actually, he did, Leyon kicked her door in. It was nice and quiet after that night for at least two years. It was a peaceful period.

TRISHA

I am Trisha Goodman. I lived in Kingstree, South Carolina for thirty- three years before I moved to New Bern, North Carolina. I met Promise's father, Arnold Toles my sophomore year of high school. Arnold was cool. He had a sweetness to him that others didn't see. The guys at school would ask what are you doing with him, Trisha? Yes, I was a church girl. My grandparents and parents were into the church. They were all ministers of the gospel in some form or another. When I was in school I got picked on. The boys always called me ugly, Chinese, or some form of the name that wasn't my government name. I like dating underdog. They didn't see you as a church girl. They saw Trisha Goodman, who was a funny, athletic, fully figure black girl. Arnold saw that but he didn't know how to embrace that part of me. His grandmother Ms. Halley. I loved her! She was the sweetest, raw truthful woman you ever wanted to meet. She knew Arnold didn't know how to treat a woman such as me. I could finish high school because of her. She kept Promise while I was in school. Ms. Halley wanted me to go off to school. She said I will take care of Promise. I knew Ms. Halley's health was failing. She didn't tell me, but I could tell. She was hanging on for Promise. She lived to see Promise at the age of thirteen. It was then I dropped out of college to focus on Promise. The promise was a beautiful young lady. Sometimes I asked God why did you give me something this beautiful. He knew I could handle every bit of it. I love my daughter. I know she thinks I didn't sometimes because I was so hard on her. I knew I had to because I didn't have anyone to consider my feelings. All I knew was to survive, and surviving isn't feelings but instinct and sacrifice. I left Arnold when I was twenty-three. A promise was maybe seven years old. When I left, Arnold it was hard but I could breathe. It was hard every step, I won't complain because God been good to me.

When I moved to New Bern, North Carolina. I thought life was going to be much better. It was before Leyon! I have always tried to be the good man what the Bible speaks of, but I kept getting the wrong hand. My grandma Anna said, "look deep before you leap." I don't understand. I looked deep, I even watched how they interacted with other people. Before I let Leyon in my house I spied on his left and right. I didn't see any signs of him being abusive. I couldn't ask his ex-wife because she was dead. I know why her ass is dead now, but anyway. He didn't have any children, well I thought. His other relatives lived out of state. I know someone spiritual probably saying baby did you pray about it?

The last person asked me that same question. I asked them "did you ask Jesus to wake you up this morning?" I heard crickets, dogs barking, and any other earthly noise with this look of she got a nerve. I had one person who answered that question. Their name is Billy Sams. Billy Sams is the minister covering for Leyon while he is in jail. He was the first man that I was attracted to mentally. His mind was so sexy to me that I would just get wet listening to his knowledge and wisdom. He had his Ph.D. in Theology but didn't make anyone feel like he was better than them. Billy embraced you. I wasn't trying to get into another relationship. I am trying to get out of Leyon way before he gets out of jail. This time away from him feels so good. I am almost moved out.

Ms. Lou son Holand moved back to the surrounding area about ten years ago after retiring from the military, the Army I think. He didn't want to settle in New Bern because the houses were too expensive. He decided to buy a house in Greenville which is about an hour away. The housing market in Greenville is cheaper than New Bern. Holand stayed in Greenville for several years until the love of his dreams came along. Ms. Lou actually like Holand's wife. Her name is Helena. Helena is a college professor at a private college in Alexandra, Virginia area. Ms. Lou explain my situation to Holand and Helena, they both agreed to let me and Promise stay there until I get on my feet. Everything is going great, that what I thought until Leyon got released from prison. He didn't let anyone know he was coming home. I will be damned! I wasn't dragging my feet for the first time. I was moving quickly but I couldn't make it obvious because the church folk and his spies would go back and tell Leyon.

When the church members would come to visit the house. I let everything look the same way Leyon left it. I wanted them to think that I was missing him. If they only knew inside I was praising God every minute for him being in jail. These people made me livid sick how they loved this demon. Leyon wasn't a man of God. Yes, God created him. He knew how to play with people's emotions. I look at Arnold and my relationship. I saw the signs but I ignored them because I was in love.

Leyon got everyone fooled except me, Promise, and Ms. Lou. After his stay in jail, he won't mess with Ms. Lou again. Ms. Lou, I love her so much. I don't know what I would've done without her. The day Leyon returned from jail. I was standing in the den looking through the kitchen window. I thought I was seeing a ghost getting out of deacon Owen's car. I ran into Promise's room to let her know Leyon was here. We were packing the last of our things. I asked God what I have done wrong. I couldn't catch a break at all. While I was rushing to get into the den, the phone began to ring. It was Ms. Lou code to let me know Leyon was back if I didn't see him. I began to sit on the sofa and cry uncontrollably. That's when I heard a knock on the kitchen door. I couldn't even hold the tears in. Leyon was thinking I was crying because I was happy to see him. I didn't want to see his black ass. I was so angry at Deacon Owen's because he had just come by here the other day. He didn't say a word to me about Leyon might be getting out early.

You could tell Leyon had lost weight while he was in jail. Leyon has always been eye candy. He is six feet, dove's dark chocolate skin tone, round face with features of the singer Babyface. Yea, he had that whip a peel for a minute. It wore off so quickly, it was like Peter and the disciples falling asleep in the garden while Jesus prayed. Do you feel me now?

I hope I can get these boxes out of here without him knowing what I am trying to do. I was so weak I couldn't move off the chair to give him a hug or any type of affection. I didn't want to give him anything but a street beat down like back in the day where you leave the boot shoe print on some part of the person's body. I would visualize that sometimes to make me happy. I remember how he would ask what I was laughing about. I would say something one of the church members said to me. I would tell him the joke only to hide the real thought of the boot shoe print. Yes, it is sad when you would praise God for that thought of beating this man to a pulp. This is what hate can do to you. I was free of him for almost two years. Damn! It is over in one day. I know he wants sex tonight. His smell of his body makes me vomit. I don't want to play that dumb trick of the disappearing magic stick. I knew where it was in my ass. It was funny he knew how to be gentle in having sex. Why he couldn't be gentle with me outside of the bedroom? Why am I asking this question when I am not going to get an answer. I have to learn to accept that now and in the future.

4

For the first time in over ten years, I cried and cried. I couldn't stop crying. I knew then all that I held inside was coming out. I was releasing all the hurt, disappointment, abuse, frustration, emotional, mental, in every form Leyon has torn me down I was finally releasing it when he walked in that door. For a full month, Leyon treated me like I was his wife and friend. In my mind, the damage is done. I don't care if you treat me like I was royalty. I can walk away and never look back. That night I went through the routine, I cooked dinner, took Promise to Halley, came back finished cleaning the dishes, and Leyon takes his shower. Something happened differently that night, I was in the kitchen finishing putting up the food when I felt a hand on my shoulder. It was Leyon's hand, massaging my shoulders, and gently kissing me on my neck. What the hell?

He hasn't done this since we got married over ten years ago. Who can I pretend I am having sex with tonight to make it through this shit? I know Paulette is getting tired of me bothering Denzel. All I can think about is Billy Sams, you are going to get your world rocked tonight. I got to tell my mind not to scream Billy's name. Billy is doing so good with the massage, he hitting places I didn't tell him where to go on my body. I know God is good! He softly turns me to kiss me so passionately that I got a chill as if my body was cold. That was my body telling me I had an orgasm without being penetrated. He whispers in my ear "you like it rough?"

"Yes!!!" I said. He grabs me and put me on the kitchen counter. He rips off my panties, lifts my skirt, and pulls me down to him. I knew Billy was going to give me the time of my life tonight. Instead, he decided to eat me, play with my clit, my body had a shock of what the hell. Billy was giving me a pleasure I haven't received in years. Billy was doing so good, that I had an orgasm that left my body limp like a crack head who had too much coke.

Billy carried me to the bedroom where he lays me on the bed so gently I thought I was on a cloud. Billy finished taking off my clothes as I laid there on the bed. He gave me another round of eating my ass. This time the orgasm was so powerful, I pasted out. I know it is the first time for everything. Billy shouldn't do me that good. I won't be able to look at him the same in the church. Billy wasn't the average size of what most men who were six to nine inches. Billy was ten and half inches maximum. His width was a half-inch. For the time, time Billy didn't ask me to put his penis in my mouth. He penetrated me for the first time in years where it didn't hurt. I had a multiple orgasms for the first time. The chemistry with Billy and me is awesome. I woke up the next morning, damn, it is Leyon.

PROMISE

An eleven-year-old girl shouldn't have to worry about my Mom. I shouldn't have to be afraid if I go back to that house Leyon might have beaten her to death. I know tonight she isn't going to be beaten. He wants sex. I know, what I know about that? I learned that one day, I was coming home from school. Mom's job had cut back her hours she would be home in the afternoons now. She worked at a local department store putting merchandise on the floor. It was like warehouse work but mom didn't care what type of work she did along I was provided for. As I was saying I came home from school I open the door quietly to make sure I didn't disturb Leyon trifflin ass studying for his sermon. I walked through the kitchen. I heard this sound like a roar. *What the hell is that?*

I moved quickly but softly to see where it was coming from. I walked down the hall and went around the corner where the guest bathroom. I saw mom and Leyon bedroom door was cracked. I peeked through and saw Mom lying there like she was motionless her mind totally somewhere else. This nut was all in it making these ugly faces.

"Baby, you drying out. I got to take care of you", said Leyon in this sensual voice. I never heard that from him. I can figure out why he isn't like that when they aren't in the bedroom. He got off the top of Mom I saw his penis. I never saw anything that big before. I was scared for

Mom. I asked Ms. Lou she explain that some men are blessed like that and others not. Leyon was blessed in that area but didn't know how to make the rest work for him. She said "if he knew how to treat her right. Tis would be skipping through New Bern like she was on a cloud. Instead, she wants to chop that penis."

All I could do was laugh because Ms. Lou spoke her mind. He got off the top of Mom and opened the nightstand side drawer. He pulled out this little bottle. He popped the lid. He points it towards Mom's vagina. Mom looked like she was enjoying him rubbing whatever it was on her vagina. He placed his fingers inside her. "T, baby that feels good. Tell me when you are coming?" said Leyon.

I was confused and disturbed for a minute. Like I said Ms. Lou gave me a quick lesson. Next, things I heard mom making this sound of relief this high pitch note as if she was warming her voice to sing. When Leyon moved his fingers from inside of her and placed them on the side of her vagina. Mom pissed in his face. Leyon was indulging in every minute of it. Mom did that twice. While Mom's back was arched and mouth was open he placed his penis in her mouth. I could hear Mom gagging so hard you could see silva running down her chin and his penis. Oh! How nasty!!

"Baby, I am ready to come......Promise be home from school soon," said Leyon.

"Yes, I'm ready Le" replied Mom. He got back on top of Mom placed it gently inside of her. Mom took a deep breath. Leyon began to move back and forth motion. He began to get a rhythm with it. Mom began to take deep breaths and her back was beginning to arch again. Leyon screams "Yes, T!!" He pulled out to let her release, as if he didn't miss a stroke. He was stroking so hard the headboard was hitting the wall like it was tapping out a coded message back in the day. "It's coming!" yelled Leyon. He made this face as if he was the "Predator" the movie and the roaring sound I heard coming in the kitchen. Once he was done releasing himself he laid on top of mom like he was weak. I moved quickly from the bedroom door. I made sure I didn't hit the place on the floor where it squeaked. I made it back out the door. I stayed at Ms. Lou's house until dinner. A course Ms. Lou called Mom to let her know I was with her. That day, I needed Ms. Lou she was the only one who could help me to understand what I saw and heard. Before I went back home, I made sure I ate at Ms. Lou's house. I couldn't look at Leyon and Mom in their faces that night. After that day, my mind was totally chopped and screwed. It didn't help that Mom and I had to be on guard. Leyon had eyes everywhere. When Leyon wanted to be alone with Mom she would bring me out here to Grandma Halley's house. This was the only place Leyon didn't know about, where I could hide safely. The people who knew I would be out here is Ms. Lou and Billy Sams. I don't know what I am going to do if Grandma died. She already did the paperwork for Mom and I to have the house when she passes on. I love it back here in the woods off from the road in the middle of Vanceboro. This became my haven and where I began to realize my talent to sing and write songs. I would sing to Grandma when she asked. She said that she could feel God's Holy Spirit glow over me when I sing songs of praise. I wasn't confident in my singing. At this time I couldn't see or think of making music or anything else as a career. I needed God to get my Mom and me away from Leyon. God, Mom didn't drag her feet. You know if we had packed up and left Leyon crew would come after us again. They made the threat that we don't want to end up like his first wife. Mom and I knew she was dead. This just confirmed that Leyon killed her. We don't have any proof. After that day, I prayed to God. He sent Billy Sams.

BILLY

I was adopted as a baby. I never knew my parents. Later, as I got about nine or ten years old, I realized I didn't look like my parents. My Mom was multi-racial and my Father was Caucasian. I was what you called a brown baby. I know I am handsome. My Mom was a Teacher and my Dad was a minister. He had his degree in Theology and didn't make anyone seem like you was below him. I know I get that from my Dad. He is an awesome man. When I finished college I told my Mom and Dad that I had to leave. I couldn't keep contact with them because they would be in danger. The only person who knew who I am was Ms. Lou. I knew Ms. Lou because my Mom and Helena are best friends. It's amazing how God work things. When I learned the truth I had to save Trisha and Promise. The problem was how when I learned of Leyon's power, it became real for sho'.

Leyon's grandfather was a part of this organization back in the day that was ruthless, let just say his grandfather wasn't the person to be messing with, if you know what I mean. This man had power that people came up missing or you had a very quick change of mind. The law enforcement was in his corner so people didn't have anyone to turn too. So, for Trisha I knew what she was going through. She didn't have anyone to help her. If Leyon found out that she was going to leave or trying to leave she would end up like my Mom. I want justice for her.

I thank God for her. Her plan is now plain. Leyon loves attention. He is like that boy in high school who was so popular that he couldn't be touched. Leyon has three children. He had his first child in college. He was accepted in Bob Jones in South Carolina. His grandfather knew some people that how he got in. The end of his freshman year he met Nancy Pamlier. Nancy was attending Clemson University. Yep, one of the top colleges in South Carolina, Leyon learned that Nancy family was very comfortable in finances. He played his cards so good that Leyon family didn't have to help him pay anything his sophomore year of college. Mr. Pamlier paid for his education. What he didn't know was Mr. Pamlier was watching him. Mr. Pamlier saw some changes in Nancy after a year of dating Leyon. Nancy wasn't happy like she was when they first dated. She seemed jumpy if anyone got to close to her. Nancy was very successful at Clemson. She had an opportunity for an internship at the beginning of her senior year of college. Leyon got her pregnant on purpose to ruin her internship. He was jealous of her success. Nancy didn't want her parents to know what Leyon had done and was doing to her. She broke up with Leyon. She told her dad about Leyon abusing her. Let's say Leyon behaved for awhile to finish out at Bob Jones because grandfather couldn't save that butt.

After he graduated from Bob Jones he got his first church in the Fayetteville, North Carolina. He met Mia Stones. Mia was a student at Methodist College. She was a church girl who didn't know about how the world plays its game. Leyon smelled it miles away. He got her pregnant andmade her give the baby up for adaptation. Mia did eventually finish her education but what Leyon did to her left a bitter taste in her mouth. Phillip Opstere grew up in the same neighborhood as Mia. Mia was out with Leyon on a regular Sunday evening service. Phillip was the musician for the guess church. He went to greet her since they haven't seen each other in years. Let say Phillip saw Leyon true colors, and got

Mia away from Leyon. Leyon didn't like that! Leyon wanted pay back. He had someone to cut Phillips break line on his car. Phillip survived the car accident but he is paralyzed from the waist down. Mia went on to marry Phillip and adapted two beautiful children. Then there is my Mom. Her name is Brenda Lemmen Bromdestin. She was amazing singer, friend and daughter. My grandparents said Leyon is good at putting on his disguise. If I knew my baby was marrying a wolf in sheep clothing I would done all I could do to stop her from marrying him. She would have still been alive. Mom was a graduate from Shaw University with a degree in Music Education. She had a voice that shook your insides. She was given the opportunity to sing with John P. Kee and Donald Lawrence when she was in Charlotte. Leyon shut that down…..oh! I hate this man. The word of God we aren't supposed to hate but love in spite of their wrong. I can do that for anyone else except Leyon. God is still helping me on that person. I am glad I am not alone on that journey.

TRISHA

I f looks could kill Leyon would be dead a long time ago. Hate shouldn't fuel you to love or to wake up every morning. In this part of my life it does. Hate keep me motivated to get away from Leyon. I remembered when I first moved to New Bern. I felt it was safe and a good place to raise Promise. I knew bad people was everywhere but I made sure the next time I would go beyond measure to make sure he was legit. Leyon was damn good at hiding his secrets. I prayed for some odd reason God didn't come in my dreams to warn me like my good friend Melinda. Melinda told me the dream of this snake coming through her wall. I knew the snake meant the enemy in spiritual terms. When she woke up from the dream, she asked God who was it? She had been dating this young man. She asked God was it this young man. She has a touch lamp on her night stand. The lamp was off. When she said that man name the lamp came on. She listened to God. She got rid of that person quick. She still desires someone special in her life but she isn't going out to find him. Melinda is a flirt. She is a comedian and very intelligent. Every woman doesn't have that quality. Enough about Melinda but I am angry at God for not warning me, at least giving me a sign in some form or another. I got nothing! I did my own undercover research, and I came up clean. What the hell? I want the person I was before he disrupts my life. I was a single mother who was happy, finally came into my talent of singing. I used to sing as a child but my love for music didn't really comealive when I was visiting a church in New Bern only a few weeks of living here. I met the woman at a car wash. I was trying to get directions to find the Windsor Apartments. She gave me the directions, and invited me to her church. Her name was Sharon Luppet. She was a member of Temple Baptist. I went the next following Sunday. I felt welcome. I was excited and passionate about music. I loved it! I began to fall asleep to music and wake up playing music. I began to get an idea of what Promise was feeling when it came to her singing. She wasn't confident in herself. I needed to get that so I could show her. I learned early that you can't tell your child or children how and why to get an education or pursue their dreams when you haven't followed that path to pursue dreams or desires. You get your child there but where and how can you tell them what to look for. You can't tell them because you won't experience the battle they experience. Yes, you may have the same feelings you experience during that battle. That spiritual battle isn't a joke. It's been several months, I have let my hate, pain, and everything else released in my singing. I started back singing in the choir. Leyon thinks it is because of him. I know it is Jesus! I was like any other Sunday morning. The choir director looked at me said lead this song because Felisha wasn't there that morning. I wasn't ready! I knew God was telling me it was time for me to bless the people with my voice. The spirit moved so high that Leyon didn't have to preach. When God bless, the enemy will mess. Leyon had something up his sleeve as soon I had gotten home. I had cooked dinner in the crock pot so it would be ready when we got home from church. Deacon Owen and his family were supposed to come over that evening to eat dinner with us. I knew something was wrong. God will reveal it soon. Leyon was happy that the Owens' didn't come because he wanted rough sex later that evening. I sent Promise to Ms. Lou's house for a few hours.

A woman shouldn't be scared to have sex with her husband. I was! Love isn't fear and fear isn't love. I don't know what getting ready to happen. I know this I haven't felt this peaceful in a long time! He has been asking me for so long to get back into the choir. My mind and ears had turned on the mute button. It is fun doing that in your mind; someone is talking to you with the facial expressions. You can't laugh so you smile. You smiling makes they think you are really taking it in but really you are telling yourself anything and everything to get through that conversation. I thank God for allowing man to create mute. For the first time I wasn't on mute anymore, it felt good. I hear the music, just as Promise did. My ideas began to flow as if I could hear a bird chirp. God would give me a melody out of that chirp. I couldn't tell everyone because people would think you were crazy. It became clear why we sing, that what I thought? Until, I was experiencing some issues going on with my vagina. This rumor of truth saying Leyon got Deacon Owen's daughter pregnant. The girl wasn't lying a course Leyon made her look like the slut of K Street. The girl was in her early twenties, she attended the local community college. She had a part time job. All she did was work, church and school. She was a typical girl where she hung out with her friends but nothing wild. I know Leyon, he saw her out besides church and she was looking good to him. She being young and naive, he talked her into having sex with him. If someone said God don't have a sense of humor. They lied!! That situation with that girl was God beginning to answer my prayers. I still had my boxes packed and ready to go hiding at Ms. Lou's house. Leyon messed up this time. See, just like he had power, Owen did too.

My vagina began to smell and have a heavy discharge. I went to see the doctor. Dr. Stendle diagnosis me with Chlamydia, which is a sexual transmitted disease. "Mrs. Goodman I am going to take some blood to check to see if you don't have anything else or serious like HIV or

AIDS", said Dr. Stendle. As I sat on that table half dressed, all I could see is RED. "Mrs. Goodman I know you are married. Did you step out on your husband? If you did we have to notify your sexual partner. You need to let them know to come in to be tested."

My eyes began to look glassy I looked Dr. Stendle in the eye and replied "I didn't go outside my marriage Dr. Stendle. This confirmed that my husband has gone outside my marriage. Two, the bruised you have seen on me that you have taken notes of all this time. My husband has been abusing for over ten years. I thank God everyday that I haven't had any children with him. If you don't see me again, please release my medical records or any other documentation for proof of my abuse. Don't say call the police or don't do anything crazy. I can't call the police because they are going to take his word over mine. My husband got people in this area thinking he is golden. He is nothing. Now, he has put my life in danger. It is time to kick rocks."

Dr. Stendle couldn't say a word because he knew it was true. He knew Leyon was abusing me. He tried to get his police buddies to look into getting me some help. Dr. Stendle and his friend family were threatened. They got a real swift of what I was trying to tell him. About two days later, I got in to see the attorney over Halley estate. I wrote my will. I wanted to make sure Promise was taken care of if I went to prison or killed. Mr. Redity knew about Leyon's power too. He saw it first hand with another situation concerning his first wife. Mr. Redity was worried because he saw something different in me this time. It scared him. He knew it wasn't anybody he could call but Billy Sams. That day Billy Sams, Promise was all late for the finale. I couldn't hear the music anymore. Because I saw rage!

PROMISE

I t began after I came from school. Leah and I walked from the bus stop at the corner of A Street and C Street. That particular day Leah wanted to go to my house to practice songs for church Sunday. Usually I go to Leah house and stay until dinner. For some reason that day was different, Leah and I walking up the street we heard a loud noise. We stopped to listen where it came from. We didn't hear it again. So we continued to walking down the street. As we got closer to the house I got this strange feeling. I couldn't describe it but it wouldn't leave me alone. I didn't say anything to Leah because I didn't want to scare her. We approached Ms. Lou's house we heard Leyon and Mom arguing. Leyon called Mom a bitch so much that she began to answer to sometimes. The cursing preacher who knew the word of God….he show didn't know in the Bible the book of Proverbs 18:22 states "He who finds a wife finds a good thing, and obtain the favor from the Lord". Leyon didn't do that with my Mom. He treated her like shit that has been wiped from a horse ass. I couldn't understand why all these years now God didn't allow him to wake up. Mom and I woke up early but now everyone else is getting ready to see what we have seen all these years. It was a voice inside of us that was rejoicing that this wolf was about to be exposed! Deacon Owen daughter was starting to show that round tummy. The phone was beginning to start to ring off the hook because the rumor is real. She is pregnant these young girls who are her friends is telling how Leyon would pick her up from school and take her to these expensive hotels and restaurants to lavish her. The day Leyon learned of her being pregnant. He tried to make her have an abortion. When she wouldn't have the abortion, Mom and I named Deacon Owens's daughter Proof. She was the proof that we needed. I guess Mom couldn't hold on any longer that day because hell broke loose for real.

As we got closer to the house this feeling got stronger, and I knew I had to get some help this time. I heard Mom scream! My heart dropped and I began to run up the street. We got to Ms. Lou house. She was already standing on the porch. She saw Leah and I running up the street, Ms. Lou yelled "P, Tis already sent the code. I called the police." I got to Ms. Lou porch threw my books on the porch. I looked at Leah to tell her to do the same. I knew this was going down today. I yelled "Ms. Lou call Billy Sams."

"I did!! He isn't answering. I don't know where he is?" she replied. I said a prayer. I gave Leah instructions to do exactly what I tell her to do. I don't have to explain now. I will later after this mess. We ran to the back of the house. The door was locked. I looked through the window. The kitchen was trashed. I could still hear them arguing. Leah gasped when she saw what the kitchen looked like. "Promise this looks like a scene from a movie."

"Leah this isn't. This is for real." I replied. I banged on the door to see if I could get their attention. I couldn't! They were so loud they couldn't hear me at all. I heard Leyon do this scrawl like a wounded dog. I knew right then my feeling just got worse. I couldn't bang on the door. I couldn't move any function of my body. Everything went still like the peace before the storm. I was in the storm at this moment. I can't hear the music.

TRISHA

The day started as any other day with Leyon. It was my day off from work. It wasn't eight o'clock in the morning yet, Deacon Owen was calling for Leyon. Proof went into premature labor about five that morning. She was going to work when she had this pain in her stomach that took her breath. The baby was moving like a jumping bean on caffeine. All I know is that Leyon was in the bed, when Owen called. Leyon got his clothes on and left for the hospital. I was praying for that baby. That baby is the answer to our prayers, all I have to do is hold on a few more months. I don't know what Owen said or did at that hospital. Leyon returned around a little after noon because I was watching the twelve o'clock news sitting in the living room. He opened the kitchen door as if he was a F5. He slammed that kitchen door so hard that I jumped. I yelled "What the hell wrong with you?"

He walked towards me like he had this fury in his eyes. I didn't know he was going to hit me, but he did! I was sitting in the love seat near the bay window in the living room. The power of that punch knocked me to the bay window. I was unconscious for awhile because when I came to myself I had a headache. I felt my face for the pain was making me aware. I was surprised to see my hand come back from my face covered in blood. I was mad as hell. I was ready to fight. I didn't see Leyon anywhere in the living room. My body is in pain. I sat myself

21

up on the floor. The realization of my left leg was not feeling like it supposed to be, it was numb from the knee to the toes. I have no other choice to call Ms. Lou. I called the first time to warn her it's Leyon. Then, I could see Leyon at the dining table in the corner near the fridge drinking a glass of Goose as if he was in pity. I said a prayer because I knew the rest of this day wasn't going to be good. I crawled to the end table near the sofa. This way Leyon couldn't see me when I was able to get to my feet. I moved very quietly and softly as if I was a plush ball rolling on the floor. This time gave me a chance to think of how I am going to get out of here. What messed me up was when I looked at the clock over it read two-forty-five. Promise will be home soon. I can't be looking like this on the floor; bleeding and can hardly move my left leg.

Leyon tried to get up because he mumbled to himself that girl on her way home. I saw him coming towards the living room. He looked by the bay window where I laid but I was no longer there. He yelled "Where are you, Bitch?" For the first time in a long time something told me I could die today. I text Ms. Lou "call the police and Billy." I hurried and put my phone in my bra. I continued to hide behind the sofa. I was waiting on my phone to vibrate in my bra to let me know Ms. Lou got the text. Just as the phone vibrated to let me know she got the text, Leyon found me behind the sofa.

"Bitch, what are you doing behind there?" he asked. I just looked at him to observe him, for the first time Leyon wasn't together. You could see he was losing his power. A man like Leyon strives off the power trip of fooling people with their persona. He got too big headed this time because Owen is NO JOKE point blank and a period. Leyon cage was rattled Proof has made him realize he couldn't get out of this mess here.

"Bitch, I know you can hear me. You better answer me now before you forget how to answer" firmly yelled Leyon. Before I could even say a word I could see the back of Leyon's left hand coming towards me. I ducked and crawled to the kitchen. I heard Leyon knock over the end table and crystal lamp my Mother gave me as my first house warming. Another sentimental piece of my life gone.....oh well, I made it to the kitchen and pull myself up on the sink. This was my attempt to see if I could put any pressure on this left leg. The result was negative. I couldn't put any pressure of that leg. Leyon hand was bloody coming towards me. I was trying to get to the kitchen door. This leg has messed me up. Leyon is coming towards me as if each step I take was being swallowed up by the earth. I slide myself to the stove. I had my cast iron skillet on the stove from cooking fried chicken the night before. I took a big stretch to get the skillet because it was on the other side of the stove. My hand was so sweaty I couldn't get a good grip on the skillet. I didn't have time to balance and adjust myself. I turned around Leyon was right there. It was perfect because I turned around swung the skillet which went right into Leyon face. I got a home run! Yay for Trisha! I continued to hold the skillet as I drugged my leg to the kitchen door. I was almost there when Leyon grabbed me by my hair. I knocked everything off the dining table by the fridge trying to swing at Leyon. I missed.....damn it! I couldn'tsee him anymore because he was behind me. I braced myself by putting my hand on the table to push off since I couldn't put any pressure on that leg. That when Leyon stabbed me in my right hand between my middle and index fingers. It was a steak knife. I pulled it out and attempted to go for the kitchen door again. Again Leyon pulled me by my hair drugged me down the hallway to the bedroom. As he was doing this to me, he called me everything except a child of God. He was blaming me for things I had never known or knew about.

"Let me go! What are you talking about Leyon? We don't have any children together. Promise isn't yours."

"Brenda, I don't want to do this but I have no choice. You are going to expose me. You knew about those documents. Where did Redity do with those papers?" he asked.

His voice had changed. He was furious not in the sense of angry. He was disturbed he was about to get caught in something that I did not know nothing about. *This is what Redity was talking about concerning Brenda. He still got the hold on Redity. If this baby comes out he loses the power. Owen takes over!* My body was introduced to the door way of our bedroom. He picked me up by the throat and threw onto the bed. I gasped for oxygen. His grip was so strong and tight I thought Lex Luger was choking Superman. Leyon stomps into the bathroom. I saw that was my attempt to get my box cutter out of my secret spot between the wall and bed of the floor. Today was the day that box cutter coming in handy. I placed the cutter under the pillow near me so it would be handy when I have to make my move. I could hear Leyon yelling and cussing while slamming cabinet doors in the bathroom. I guess he finally found what he was looking for because I could hear bottles and things hitting the floor, sink and counter. He came out of the bathroom with a bottle of Ciroc vodka not open, a bottle of pills, and a thirty-eight.

My shirt was ripped from where he drugged me down the hallway. Leyon had this look like he was aroused by bra and breast being exposed. He continued to yell and cuss as he laid the Ciroc, the pills and the thirty-eight on the night stand.

"You are going to give me some of that pussy, Bitch"

"Hell No! Mother Fucker" I yelled and attempt to kick him in the balls while he was over me. I knew he was going to go for my pants first. I was so damn mad at myself for missing those balls. I was going to stomp the shit out of those nuts. Leyon response to my retaliation he punched me in my left leg. I knew I was going to kill his ass, the mercy was gone. I have to calm down enough to find out why Leyon killed Brenda. I took the pain the best way I could.

"Bitch I am going to give you the opportunity to take your clothes off willingly. If you don't corporate, I will take them off myself and beat the hell out of you while I get my pussy" he said enduringly calm.

I replied "No! I am not taking off my clothes. If you touch one piece of clothes on me, today will be your last day on earth."

"Bitch, you don't scare me. You ain't going to do shit" he yelled. He leaned over and grabbed for my pants. I kicked him in the chest; which caused him to stumble backwards, when he got his balance he stood up as if he was the Incredible Hulk.

"That doesn't scare me!" I said.

He rips open his pants, took them off and slams them to the floor. You could see thru his boxers that he had a hard on. He rushes towards me and grabs both of my legs. I screamed from the pain of my left leg.

"Bitch, I thought you were strong" he chuckled. He took off my pants and ripped my panties. He threw everything to the other side of the bed. Leyon penis looked bigger than usually. I knew I couldn't let him completely rape me today. I've been forced to have sex with him too many times. Then, he had the nerve to give me an STD. OH Hell NO! I knew once he gets into the pussy he would forget on being aware. I have to behave to get the information about Brenda. Also, I need to keep my hands free to get the cutter from under the pillow.

Once he penetrated me he purred like a kitten. I was screaming in my head get the hell off of me! I was observing his body. He was about to get that first orgasm.

"Leyon who is your baby?" I asked in a sensual tone.

"Brenda is her name and she knew how to play the game" he replied.

"Who knows all about you, Leyon?"

"Brenda, you know more about me than anyone else. Sorry, I had to do this. I didn't have any choice. Nancy couldn't know what I've done to our child"

Leyon was about at his peak. I knew I had to put some energy into this to get him to lean in closer so I could cut or stab him. While his eyes were rolling back in his head, I eased my box cutter from under the pillow. I held it inside my hand. His ritual is when he gets an orgasm. He kisses me very passionately. It was his way to say thank you. Leyon was the type of man who would get an orgasm and keep it movin' if you know what I mean until the ultimate orgasm presented itself. I could see the goose bumps that looked like measles beginning to pop out from his shoulders. It was time for me to count down before he kisses me. 10, 9, 8, 7, 6, 5, 4, he leans in for the kiss I execute my stab in the neck, blood squirts all over me. I push him off. I rolled to the edge of the bed and lands on my right foot. I hopped to the bedroom door as if I was in a one legit race. I didn't have any time. I could hear the sirens coming closer. I hopped to the end of the hallway. I looked at the kitchen door. I saw Promise standing in this blank stare. Leah standing next to her crying like it was the end of the world. I hopped to the kitchen door. Promise couldn't believe I was there in from of her. I told Promise and Leah let's move quickly and get to Ms. Lou's house. About that time I saw Billy Sam's car coming up the street. He had our hidden bags from Ms. Lou's house in the car. He helped me get in the car. Billy drove until we didn't have any choice to stop and rest.

Billy

As I approached the Virginia state line, I knew my body was getting tired. Trisha's leg and hand needed to get medical attention. I had to make a phone call. I knew who could help me to get Trisha some help. I haven't talked to this person in years. Her name is Alessia Famise. I met Alessia when I was finding my way in life. She was going to school to be an RN. Now, its five years later she is a RN, divorced, single Mom and last time I checked she was almost done going back to school as a Nurse Practioner. Alessia is an awesome woman. *That ex-husband needed his ass kicked....sorry Jesus. That wasn't the proper language. Yes, I don't have any room to judge because you are judge and jury. Please weight the scales in her favor. What I never told Alessia was I loved her. I was so in love with her that I would see her favorite color blue. My eyes would water up.* I saw the sign that said "Welcome to Danville". We are in Virginia. Danville was a sleepy town in the hill side of the Blue Ridge Mountains. It was beautiful driving in the country side. The roads were hilly and curvy. You enjoyed the view as if you were on top of the mountain. I have to stop to make this phone call to Alessia. Trisha, Promise and Leah were all asleep. My hands were so sweaty that I could hardly hold the stirring wheel too easy to the side of the road. I drove to the top of the hill and could see a cellular tower about a hundred feet from the house. I could see an open field across the street it has a wooden path, just in case we are being on watched I will park there to use the phone. As I turned the car into the path, I could hear Alessia voice in my head. Her voice is so sensorial that I melt when she answer the phone. For years I have called to hear her voice and hanged up the phone. I know it sounds stupid but I couldn't put her in danger while Leyon was living. Now, that he is dead. It is a whole another story. I parked the car where I think it was good enough to not be seen. I gently open the car door. I walked a few inches away from the car. I pulled my cell phone out of my pocket. I took a deep breath; I began to dial her number. I waited for the phone call to be connected I begin to feel butterflies in my stomach. I heard the phone ring three times. Then there was the voice that made me melt in my shoes.

"Hello, Hello, Hello"

"Hello. Alessia" I replied.

"Billy is that you?" she asked. I could feel her smiling through the phone.

"Yes, Alessia. How are you?"

"I am fine. A little better that I am talking to you"

"O! Really!" At this moment I sounded like a girl who just got the answer she was expecting. I had to regroup. "Sorry about that I am glad I made your day." That is better Sam. I could hear her chuckle. Her chuckle had the uniqueness that sound like a pig squall. I always thought it was cute to me.

"What's up, Billy?" she asked.

"Alessia, I need your help. Remember I told you I couldn't get into a serious relationship until I take care of something that won't come back and bite me later."

"Yes, what happened?" she asked.

"Well, it didn't go the way it seemed. I have a friend. Her husband abused her. I think her leg is broken and he stabbed her in the hand. She really needs medical attention. Can you get someone to check her out? Next, I need you to bring me the Tahoe. They are going to be looking for my Volvo Wagon. Once she gets medical attention we all have to get back on the road."

"Where are you?" she asked.

"I am by the farmhouse down the hill by the open field where we used to meet late at night."

"Billy, I thought about that night several times. I............I will be there in twenty minutes."

I hung up the phone, slowly walked to the car. I could see Trisha sleeping so peaceful. She was smiling in her sleep. I didn't want to disturb her. I couldn't imagine being with someone like Leyon for over ten years and can't enjoy true happiness.

"Trish, wake up. Trish, wake up" said calmly. Her eyes closed I see her eyes moving. I saw the tear running on the side of her face. I grabbed and hugged her so tight that I could feel her heartbeat. Trish, completely fell apart. She wasn't trying to be loud because she put the sleeve of my shirt over her mouth so Promise and Leah wouldn't hear her. I knew Leyon had done some real damage to this woman. Leyon needed his tail whooped for all the lives he has killed. Trisha continued to just cry her eyes out. It was like she didn't know how to stop. Her body was on autopilot. I knew all the hurt, abuse, and turmoil Leyon had done she was now free. This is including the pain of her hand and leg. All I could do was hold her. I let her know she was safe with me. The more I said she was safe the harder Trisha would cry. I could begin to see Promise and Leah awaking. I called out to them to wake up. I gave them instructions on to clean out the car, take off the license plate, and any other information that could link them to the car. After I gave Promise and Leah the instructions they got moving quickly. These girls are productive. I saw Alessia pulling up. Before Alessia could pull up the car trunk, glove compartment, under and back seats were cleaned out. I carried Trisha in my arms to the car. She was still crying. Promise stayed with Trisha, while Leah, Alessia and I put everything in the back of the Tahoe. Leah climbed into the third row from the back. I jumped into the drive seat, while Alessia had this look in her eyes that she would "ride and die" with and for me.

"Lessia, does Joe know we are coming?" I asked softly.

"Yes, as soon I got off the phone with you. I called. All he said was "its time". What does that mean Billy?"

I gave her this curious look, but I didn't know where to begin. I braced myself to say "Joe witnessed a murder. He is my uncle." Trisha stops crying long enough to scream "Brenda had a brother".

"Yes, Trisha" I replied.

"Why you never told me Joe was your uncle Billy?" asked Alessia.

"I couldn't tell you because we had to live our life in secret as long Leyon Bromdestin was alive. It was dangerous. When we get to Joe's I got to call Redity. Right now let's get Trisha taken care of. Alessia, do you know a doctor who you can trust with helping us."

"Yes, he is going to meet us at the clinic. I gave him the instructions on what to do once he gets to the clinic. Billy, we are covered."

"I hope so. We don't need any screw ups. How far do we have before we get to the clinic?" I asked.

"It is just up the road about ten minutes. Trisha is you in a lot of pain?"

"Yes! I can't put any pressure on the leg. It is very swollen" replied Trisha.

"Trisha, I think your leg is broken, like Billy thought"

We approached the road to turn onto the clinic. I could see other cars around.

"Alessia, who are these cars?" I asked.

"I don't know! Nobody supposed to be here except the doctor. Hold on let me call him." She pulled her phone out of her shirt pocket. She continues to dial the doctor number. He took a while to answer the phone.

"Alessia, something is wrong? I can feel it. You try calling again. Do the, b, c, d test. Do you remember?"

"Yes, I think A is all clear, B is boating mean wait, C is coasting means take your time and D is dog mean dangerous."

"You got it! Joe doesn't like dogs. That is why we use dog for dangerous. Alessia, try calling again if he don't answer we are going to move from this hiding spot."

Alessia picked up her phone to try to call again. The call connected it felt like we were waiting on a death sentence. The second ring no answer. The third ring no answer. The fourth ring "Hello Alessia."

"Doc, are you ok?" she asked.

"Yea, why?"

"Why didn't you answer the phone earlier? I was in the back working on some paperwork."

"Ok. Who is the apple car?" she asked.

"I don't know"

"Did Ray go on the boating trip with her boyfriend?"

"No"

"Did August go with April on the cruise?"

"Yes, he called for her. Didn't know who was taking care of the dog."

"Ok. Until we meet again, friend. I love you." Before she could hang up, she heard the bullet. She screamed! "Billy, I have to go get Thomas."

"Where is he?"

"He is at the babysitters" with a shaky voice she cried for her friend. She knew it could've been her. "Billy, this just got real."

"Yes, Alessia. I told you. When you go in to pick up Thomas, don't show any emotion. You need to get yourself together. You are going to have to put life on hold. You need to tell your family they are in danger. Let them know this isn't a joke. Give them the instructions to go to Delaware. Do you understand me?"

"Yes, Billy."

As Alessia picked up Thomas from the babysitter, the babysitter Ms. Anne wanted to chat. I was watching from the Tahoe. Ms. Anne husband die over eight years ago. She is moody because he was rocking that world. She gets lonely and wants to talk. Alessia need to let Ms. Anne know today is not the day. Alessia come on…..ten, nine, eight, seven, six, five, four, three, ok Alessia is out the door. She was watching her surrounding while she was walking to the car. Once she entered the car, Alessia handed the baby to Promise. Promise handed Thomas to Leah. Leah wasknown to a car seat. She was active with the children ministry in church. She was excited to see a baby. Alessia just cried. This time the roles were reversed. Trisha was lending out her hand instead someone lending a hand to her.

PROMISE

I knew this day would come. I just think it was going to happen before the baby got here. It doesn't seem real that Leyon is dead. Yay! Lord forgives me. I shouldn't be doing this. God it could've been my Mom. Now, we on our way to Delaware, I feel sad for Alessia. Her world just got turned upside down. When she called her parents, they said some awful things to her. Billy was a good man. He stood up to her parents. That changed quick when they realized it was Billy Sams. They shut up and followed his instructions. Billy is frustrated because we are down to a thousand dollars. We spent two hundred to make sure the baby is ok with formula and pampers for awhile once we get to Joe's. We have another six hours to go. I know I am hungry at this present moment. I am not going to say nothing because Billy is already stressed trying to figure out how to make this money last with gas and food. While I see Billy Sams stressed for the first time. I see my Mom connecting with Alessia. WOW! She hasn't connected or spoken to another soul like this in years. I guess she felt there was no one she could trust with what Leyon has done to her all those years besides Ms. Lou. Mom and Ms. Lou showed made sure that if anything happen they made sure they had some form of DNA to show that the baby was Leyon. Once a month Leyon liked for Mom to cut his nose hairs, well the last time mom did cut them. Leyon was in a rush to get somewhere.

Well, Mom put those clippings into a little Ziplocbag; put them inside my bookbag to drop off to Ms. Lou for safe keepings. I know Ms. Lou is getting the third degree from Mr. Redity. Owen won't touch Ms. Lou. I don't know why but he won't. This organization code is distinctive. What I meant by that is they have a part that goes like if they have an enemy among the brothers, no one outside the organization can't kill him for no reason at all. That brother can kill him for justice call. So, we didn't have a choice to run. Owen was going to have mom killed, if we stayed to fight it out. I am glad God sent Billy Sams to help us. Never thought the person who supposes to give us the word of God would also be the angel too. He told Mom and me about Joe. He didn't say it was his Uncle. I remembered when I first saw Joe picture. He was much younger. Joe looked like he was in his late twenties. He was fine, Lawd! I seen older men who looked well for their ages but Joe I was curious. I was attracted to Joe just seeing his picture. This never happened to me before. I can't say anything but I am so ready to see him. If I say anything to anyone they going to say I have a crush on Joe. Oh how cute.......Damn it! This isn't a crush. I knew that from day one I laid my eyes on that picture. Yes, I am fourteen. No, this isn't the love where I want to give honor to God for my life, health and strength. I really want Joe to make love to me. Yea, yea, what I know about sex I don't. I never had sex. I am still a virgin. That experience watching Mom and Leyon I knew what to do and not to do. I think that says enough for that. After seeing what type of man my own Father was and how Leyon treated my Mom. I was determined to have what I wanted and needed. If it was Joe, fine. If it wasn't oh well I will keep it moving until God send the right one. First, I have to work on me and my goals.

"Promise, what are you thinking about? I can see it all over your face" asked Leah

"I was thinking about what Ms. Lou was doing. If it is Saturday she is going to be sitting on that porch early in the morning to watch the sun come up. She wanted to greet Jesus in the morning that how she greeted him by waiting on him" I replied.

"Ms. Lou is a mess and a mystery. I miss my friend" replied Mom.

My mom is back. Words can't not express or describe how pain and hurt can make you feel after receiving it again and again. It comes in different forms but it feels the same. The feeling is numbness. You don't want to deal or live in this society of people God created. You see a person comes towards you. Your questions in your head is what do they want? What is their motive? If it not the questions, then you say to yourself leave me alone, go away, I don't want to be bothered with you. That is how I feel and has felt this way towards people. You are so burnt out with being hurt or just dealing with people period that you are so glad to get in your home because it is your space where you can control your atmosphere. You might say you can control your atmosphere where ever you are. It doesn't work like that always. I don't work a job but when I am at school. The teacher is in control of the classroom. She is in control so I have to follow her rules. I would love to tell her leave me alone, shut the hell up and I will do the work later. It doesn't work that way. I can't imagine what my Mom has felt over ten years. At one time I wondered if she felt anything. I knew she loved me. I didn't have a clue how she felt for Ms. Lou. She expressed her feelings for the first time in over ten years. When Grandma Halley died, Mom didn't even cry. She didn't even cry at the funeral. Leyon had emotionally shaken her dry. Even though we are over this hump yet, mom looks so good. She has a different look about her. I can't explain it. I am so happy. My mom is coming back to me.

LEYON

I'm sorry. I can't go back and change things now. I made my decision. In hell, I have lifted my eyes. I know what the Bible had said that he would depart me from I know you not. That is what I have heard, when he looked in that book of Life. I knew what God was going to say. It began when I was a little boy. My grandparents raised me while my parents worked. Grandma Lamona and Granddaddy Lee was an odd couple. Grandma said there was days she could she would. I did not understand then, but I do now. I loved my grandparents especially my grandfather. He was so well respected in the community. I thought it was because he was a deacon in the church, active in community organizations and he would help anyone. It wasn't because he was an upright man. My grandfather was like the head of a mafia. He groomed the men out of the church to be a part of his organization. I was fifteen when my grandfather health started to fail. He always told me when the time is right he would show me. Well, he did! On my sixteenth birthday, my grandfather told me to meet him at the house. Grandma begged him not to do this. I never forget it she said "Lee, let it go! Repent to God and let it go. Don't make this baby loose his soul because of you."

My grandfather pushed my grandma out of the way of the door. I was about to defend her until I looked into my grandfather eyes. They looked possessed. I was afraid. What I felt was undescribed. That night

I saw a man get beat to death and these men dispose of the body. My grandfather let me know I couldn't tell no one what I experienced that night. When my Mother figured out why behavior had change. It was too late. I oversaw the organization. I couldn't let my grandfather down. Yes, I knew right from wrong. I wanted to please him so badly that I lost my soul. I know I'm sorry is too late.

I loved Brenda and Trisha so much. My anger caused me to kill Brenda and I children so many times I can't count. When Brenda was gone for almost a year I knew she was up to something but the spy I had on her couldn't uncover what she had planned. This was when I became angry with Brenda. She was better at the game than me now. Plus, she had the master skill men in her family. It wasn't too long after she returned home I killed her. She wouldn't tell me what she was doing while she was away. She told me God knew.

He did! I still don't know. I was single for almost eight years before Trisha came into town. You can tell she had innocents that was pure. I tried breaking it because she had a relationship with God and Ms. Lou. She won!

JOE

My name is Joseph John Lemmen. My sister was Brenda Lemmen Bromdestin. Leyon met Brenda through me. When I went off to college I wasn't sure what I wanted to do. After all my trial and errors, I came back to music. I received my degree from Fayetteville State University. Later, I received my Masters from Shaw University. During that time Leyon didn't show the colors of evilness. He showed all the fruits of the spirit. He always showed peace and happiness. I thought his life was golden. Well, about ten years after I received my Masters degree, this opportunity to go on tour with a big gospel artist by the name of Peter Robrams. He loved my skills of playing the piano and drums. Robrams offered me the position on the spot. At the time, Shelly Deems was my girl then, during that time we dated for two years. She was ready to be married. Not me! I wanted to get a little more stable in my music career. Shelly was showing her true colors. Like Grandma Ellamor would say "showing her ass", she was my dad mother. She knew about God but she would let her flesh win when someone made her mad. Anyway, Shelly showed her ass at six months pregnant. One day she was stressing me out so good, I just mentally shut down. I didn't want to see no body, no forms of human creatures. I was like this for three days. On the fourth day, Leyon dropped by to see me. He told me about a brotherly Christian organization. They called it BC. It stood for Brotherly Combat. Leyon made it seem it was like a Big Brother, Big Sister Organization or like a mentor one on one. Leyon was embedded from his grandfather to his generation. Once I went to the Saturday meetings, they have at any local church where a member of the group attends. I confided about Shelly on Saturday evening. By Sunday Shelly was gone MIA. I have never seen her again. I do have a son. His name is Payne. I never met my son. After they did this for me I was supposed to do whatever they asked of me. I did my first assignment I know it was wrong. God said in his word 'revenge is mine saith the Lord'. I did so well on my first assignment. Leyon made me one of the top reporters. My music career had begun to taking off again. I saw a difference in my sister. She would never tell me. My spirit knew what Leyon was doing. I kept myself under control. Even though, I wanted to beat the cramp out of Leyon. Brenda came to me when she found out she was pregnant with Billy. Mr. Redity did the papers for the adoption. Ms. Lou knew about the organization because that is how her husband disappeared. Ms. Lou could never be touched because she had me and proof of the crime that BC committed. Leyon though he got away killing my sister. Thank God for Trisha! He won't call no one else bitch. My goal is to keep Promise and Trisha safe from BC. My sister death gave me a new light. I wasn't supposed to get out of BC alive. I knew too much, has done too much to survive. God grace and mercy is awesome. Roman 6:14 states "sin shall not be your master, because you are not under law, but under grace". This is what I've stand upon. I'm not under Leyon or Owen anymore! I'm under God. He is what rules me. I am my brother's keeper. This is my first assignment of doing what God requires of me. Only then after the assignment is completed, I will hear the music again.

Printed in the United States
by Baker & Taylor Publisher Services